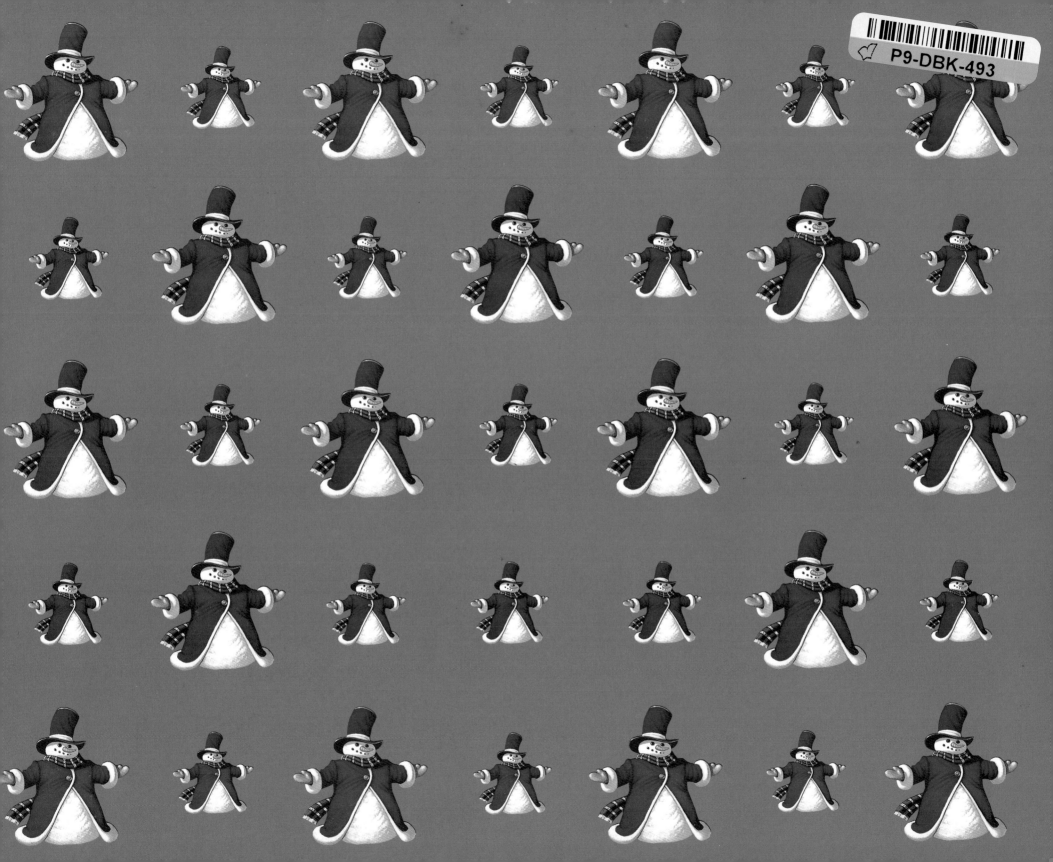

SANTA'S TWIN

By **DEAN KOONTZ**
Illustrations by **PHIL PARKS**

HarperPrism
An Imprint of HarperPaperbacks

Copyright © 1996 by Dean Koontz
Cover and interior illustrations © 1996 by Phil Parks
All rights reserved.

HarperPrism is an imprint of HarperPaperbacks.
First printing: November 1996
Designed by: Lili Schwartz

Visit HarperPaperbacks on the World Wide Web at
http://www.harpercollins.com/paperbacks

Library of Congress Cataloging-in-Publication Data
is available from the publisher.

Printed in China

❖ 10 9 8 7 6 5 4 3 2 1

*To Gerda, as a reminder of our first
Christmas, when it snowed just for us, and
the best gift was being together.*
—Dean Koontz

*To my children—Joel, Amanda, and
Bethany—who have helped me remember
the magic and love of Christmas.*
—Phil Parks

Well, now Thanksgiving is safely past,
more turkey eaten this year than last,
more stuffing stuffed, more yams jammed
into our mouths, and using both hands,
coleslaw in slews, biscuits by twos,
all of us too fat to fit in our shoes.

So let's look ahead to the big holiday
that's coming, coming, coming our way.
I'm sure you know just what day I mean.
It's not Easter Sunday, not Halloween.
It's not a day to be sad or listless.
It's a day of wonder. It's Christmas!

Charlotte and Emily love this season.
They're kids, so they have good reason
to dream all year of that special eve
because they truly and deeply believe
a gift-giving fat man flies the sky,
with toys and goodies galore. No lie!

He'll soon be up there and on his way
in a maximum-cool, cherry-red sleigh
with camouflage stars on the underside,
taking the wildest of all thrill rides,
like a roller coaster on tracks of air,
pulled by reindeer harnessed in pairs.

So someday soon, they'll put up a tree.
Why only one? Maybe two, maybe three!
Deck it with tinsel and baubles bright.
It'll be an amazing and wonderful sight.
String colored lights out on the roof—
pray none are broken by anything's hoof.

Salt down the shingles to melt the ice.
If Santa fell, it just wouldn't be nice.
He might fracture his leg or even be cut,
perhaps even break his big jolly butt.
They don't want Santa's butt in a sling.
What a ghastly, bad, unthinkable thing.

Oh, wait! I just heard terrible news.
Hope it won't give you Christmas blues.
Santa was mugged, tied up, and gagged,
blindfolded, ear-stoppled, and bagged,
locked in his cellar under the Pole,
down in a dismal, deep, dark, dank hole.

His sleigh is waiting out in his yard,
and someone has stolen Santa's bank card.
Soon his accounts will be picked clean
by the use of automatic-teller machines.
And what will happen to all the toys
made as gifts for good girls and boys?

$\mathcal{H}$ark! The sound of silver sleigh bells
echoes high over the hills and the dells.
And look—reindeer far up in the sky!
Some silly goose has taught them to fly.
The driver giggles quite like a loon—
a madman, a goofball, a thug, or a goon.

Something is wrong—any fool could tell.
If this is Santa, then Santa's not well.
His mean little eyes spin just like tops.
So somebody better quick call the cops!

A closer look confirms his psychosis.
And—oh, my dear—really *bad* halitosis.
Beware when Christmas comes this year,
because there's something new to fear.
Santa's twin—who is rude and mean—
stole the sleigh, will make the scene.

He's pretending to be his good brother.
Guard your beloved children, Mother!
Down the chimney and into your home,
here comes that deeply troubled gnome.

Reindeer sweep down out of the night.
See how each is brimming with fright?
Tossing their heads, rolling their eyes,
these gentle animals are all so wise—
they know this Santa isn't their friend,
but an imposter and far 'round the bend.

They would stampede for all they're worth,
dump this nut off the edge of the earth.
But Santa's bad brother carries a whip,
a club, a chocolate-cream pie at his hip,
a blackjack, spitballs—you better run!—
and a fearful, horrible, wicked ray gun.

They land on the roof, quiet and sneaky.
Oh, but this Santa is fearfully freaky.
He whispers a warning to each reindeer,
leaning close to make sure they hear:
"You have relatives back at the Pole—
antlered, gentle, quite innocent souls.

"So if you fly off while I'm inside,
back to the Pole on a plane I will ride.
I'll have a picnic in the midnight sun:
reindeer pie, pâté, reindeer in a bun,
reindeer salad, and hot reindeer soup,
oh, all sorts of tasty reindeer goop."

$\mathcal{A}$t the chimney, he looks down the bricks.
But that entrance is strictly for hicks.
With all his tools, a way in can be found
for a fat, bearded burglar out on the town.

From roof to backyard to the kitchen door,
he chuckles about what he has in store
for the good family that's sleeping within.
He grins his biggest and nastiest grin.
Oh, what a creep, what a scum and a louse.
He's boldly breaking into their house!

With picks, loids, gwizzels, and zocks,
he quickly and silently opens both locks.
He enters the kitchen without a sound.
Now chances for devilment truly abound.

He opens the fridge and eats all the cake,
pondering what sort of mess he can make.
First he pours milk all over the floor,
pickles, pudding, and ketchup—and more!
He scatters the bread—white and rye—
and finally he spits right into the pie.

At the corkboard by the phone and stool,
he sees drawings the kids did at school.
Emily has painted a kind, smiling face.
Charlotte has drawn elephants in space.

The villain takes out a red felt-tip pen,
taps it, uncaps it, chuckles, and then,
on both pictures, scrawls the word "Poo!"
He always knows the *worst* things to do.

His mad giggles continue to bubble,
while he gets into far greater trouble.
He's hugely more evil than he is brave,
so then, after he loads up the microwave

with ten whole pounds of popping corn
(oh, we should rue the day he was born),
he turns and runs right out of the room,
because that old oven is gonna go BOOM!

He prowls the downstairs—wicked, mean—
looking to cause yet one more bad scene.
When he sees the presents under the tree,
he says, "Time for a gift-swapping spree!
I'll take out all the really good stuff,
then box up dead fish, cat poop, and fluff.

"In the morning these kiddies will find
coffee grounds, peach pits, orange rinds,
old stones, mud pies, and rotten potatoes,
hairballs, dead fish, and spoiled tomatoes.
Instead of nice sweaters, games, and toys,
they'll get slimy stinky stuff that annoys."

Charlotte and Emmy are up in their beds,
dreams of Christmas filling their heads.
Suddenly a sound startles these sleepers.
They sit up in bed and open their peepers.
Nothing should be stirring, not one mouse,
but the girls sense a villain in the house.

You can call it psychic, a hunch, osmosis,
or maybe they smell the troll's halitosis.
They leap out of bed, forgetting slippers,
two brave and foolhardy little nippers.
"Something's amiss," young Emily whispers.
But they can handle it—they're sisters!

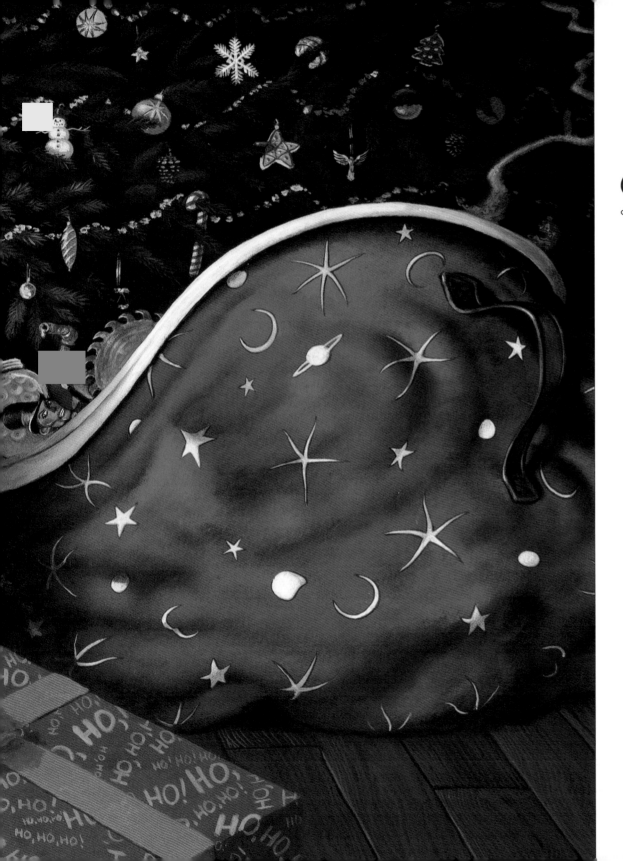

Down in the living room, under the tree,
Santa's evil twin is chortling with glee.
He's got a collection of gift replacements
taken from dumps, sewers, and basements.

He replaces a nice watch meant for Lottie
with a nasty gift for a girl who's naughty,
which is one thing Lottie has never been.
Forgetting her vitamins is her biggest sin.

In place of the watch, he wraps up a clot
of horrid, glistening, greenish toad snot.
From a package for Emily, he steals a doll
and gives her a new gift sure to appall.

It's slimy, rancid, and starting to fizz.
Not even the villain knows what it is.
The stink could stop a big runaway truck,
it's such gooey, gluey, woozy-making muck.

In jammies, slipperless, now on the prowl,
the girls go looking for whatever's foul.
Right to the top of the stairs they zoom,
making less noise than moths in a tomb.

They're both so delicate, slim, and petite,
and both of them have such tiny pink feet.
How can these small girls hope to fight
a Santa who's liable to kick and to bite,
who has a chocolate-cream pie for throwing,
and a fearful ray gun that's softly glowing?

Are these girls trained in tae kwon do?
No, no, I'm afraid that the answer is no.
Grenades tucked in their jammie pockets?
Lasers implanted inside their eye sockets?
No, no, I'm afraid that the answer is no.
Yet down, down the shadowy stairs they go.

The danger below, they can't comprehend.
This Santa has gone far round the bend.
He's meaner than flu, toothaches, blisters.
But they're tough too—they're sisters.

In the front room, at one of the trees
the bad twin of Santa is on his knees,
giggling as he stuffs another gift box
with a few pairs of his smelly old socks.
He snorts and he chortles with evil glee
and mutters, "No one will know it was me.

"They'll blame my brother, Chris Kringle,
and then next Christmas the merry jingle
of sleigh bells will alarm and terrorize.
Every little kid will watch the skies
and scream aloud when the sleigh appears.
Oh, for one hundred or *two* hundred years,

"Santa Claus will be feared, distrusted,
because everyone will still be disgusted
by all the tricks that I play this night.
They'll never forgive the harm and fright.
The toad snot and snail spit! The slime!
This scheme of mine is superb, sublime!

"The gift-wrapped broccoli and the spinach!
Oh, my goody-goody brother is finished.
Brussel-sprouts candy and unsweetened yams,
Chicken-gizzard jelly! Lima-bean jams!
Boxes full of spiders, worms, and bugs!
Old Santa won't be getting any more hugs.

Instead, kids will scream, run, and hide,
and not one child on the earth will abide
the sight of his jolly, merry old face.
The cops will be hunting him everyplace.

"Searching alleys, cellars, and attics
from tropical jungles up to the Arctic.
If they jail him—won't that be funny?
Then I'll go after the Easter bunny!"

From the doorway, the girls have heard
every shocking, horrid, despicable word.
Christmas is now theirs alone to save.
They must be bold. They must be brave.
The troll left his ray gun out of reach.
Emmy sneaks to it. Isn't she a peach?

Lottie makes fists of her small hands.
Oh, the time has come to make a stand.
Holding the ray gun, Emmy says, "Freeze!"
The troll insists: "Better say 'please.'"

He rises—a giant. He turns and growls.
He hisses, grumbles, and softly howls.
His eyes spin. His nose spouts steam.
He's a Santa monster from a bad dream,
capering, threatening: "Booga-ooga-boo!"
Lottie says, "We aren't scared of you."

The elf declares, "I eat kids for lunch.
I eat 'em for breakfast—by the bunch.
Sometimes I eat children for supper too,
baked in a crust or cooked in a stew."

Lottie says, "Listen, mister, you framed
your brother, and you oughta be ashamed."
Waving the ray gun, young Emmy commands,
"Up with your hands, up with your hands!

"This alien weapon will turn you to dust.
Or maybe to cinders. Or maybe to rust.
Or maybe to cornflakes or maybe to mice.
Whatever it does, I'm sure it's not nice."

The troll is not merely evil but quick.
Up his big sleeve he has one more trick.
From his hip holster he suddenly draws
a chocolate-cream pie. He knows no laws.

He's a gangster, a thug, a bad boy indeed,
and he flings the pie with fearful speed.
Lottie studies ballet and has some grace.
She spins—but still gets pie in the face.

Emmy fires the ray gun. Oh, no! Oh, no!
The living room magically fills with snow.
It's a weather gun, some strange device.
The fireplace mantel is all hung with ice.
From out of the ceiling a blizzard falls,
drifting over furniture and up the walls.

The malevolent elf can't repress a giggle.
"From this one, child, you cannot wriggle.
For this big mess, you won't be thanked.
In fact, I bet you're gonna get spanked.
Spanked so hard that your ears will slip
all the way down, down, down to your lips."

Then instead of cooking them in a stew
or brewing some tasty little-girl brew,
the giggling troll flees into the night.
The girls give chase, 'cause it isn't right
that he should be allowed to skip and run
after ruining Christmas, spoiling the fun.

Like many bullies, he's bluster and bluff.
He's not really made of very stern stuff.
The two girls chase him out the front door.
He slip-slides across the icy porch floor,
falls down the steps, flat on the ground,
and lands with a rubbery, blubbery sound.

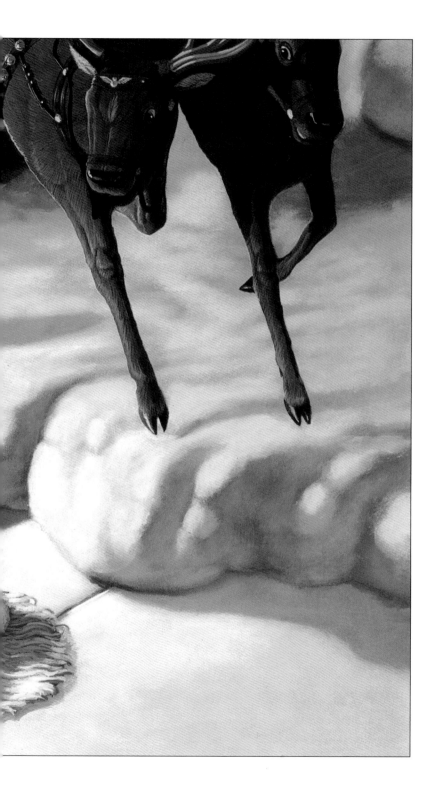

The sisters run barefoot into the snow
to make sure he doesn't jump up and go.
"Knocked himself silly. What'll we do?"
asks Charlotte as her pink feet turn blue.

Suddenly eight reindeer descend from above,
each deer flying with the grace of a dove
to the snowy lawn in front of the house,
making less sound than one wary mouse.

A deer says, "Christmas mustn't be bleak."
Emmy gasps, "Since when do reindeer speak?"
"Magical reindeer," Charlotte supposes.
In agreement the deer twitch their noses.

One reindeer licks at Charlotte's face
and says, "My, what a very unusual place
to find chocolate pudding Christmas night."
Lottie replies, "I was in a pie fight."

$\mathcal{G}$irls, you must come with us to the Pole.
Santa's in a dismal, deep, dark, dank hole.
We've deliveries to make—games and toys—
to millions and millions of girls and boys."

The sisters aren't dressed for the Pole
or for any dismal, deep, dark, dank hole.
So the reindeer wiggle their magic snoots,
and now the girls are standing in boots.

$\mathcal{P}$ajamas transform into snowsuits of red,
nothing at all like what they wore to bed.
Woolen mittens, long scarves, jaunty caps,
"What about a driver's license and maps?"

"No maps are needed," or so the deer say.
"No license required to drive *this* sleigh—
just a lot of faith and a good pure heart.
That's all that you need to do your part."

$\mathcal{T}$hey have a problem with Santa's bad twin,
who's flat on the ground on belly and chin.
He's knocked out cold. Wow, does he snore!
Loading him into the sleigh—what a chore.

First the old troll must be tied up tight
to prevent trouble the rest of the night.
They bind him fast with jump ropes and Slinkys
and tie his long mustache to his pinkies.

Lifting him into the sleigh—they'll fail,
because he weighs half as much as a whale.
Reindeer noses twitch—the magic is back.
Something stirs in the *real* Santa's sack.

Teddy bears, stuffed dogs, toy monkeys too:
all spring to life. It's a magical zoo.
They help the girls load up the evil Claus,
using their hands, their tails, their paws.

With huffing and puffing the job gets done,
although heaving an evil Claus is no fun.
The last toy returns to the sack with a wave,
and Lottie grabs the reins. She's so brave!

In the sleigh Emmy sits by her sister's side
and says to the deer, "Let's start this ride.
To the top of the world! Up, up in the sky!
Let's see if reindeer really know how to fly."

Up into the night the eight reindeer spring.
The bells on their harnesses all softly ring.
Up toward the stars and the big frosty moon.
Charlotte says, "I think I'm going to swoon."

"No, no," says Emmy, "we must save Saint Nick.
And I think I might possibly be getting sick.
I'm so woozy, and my head's spinning around.
Oh, I've just *got* to hold my cookies down."

$\mathcal{R}$eindeer are flyers of fabulous skill.
Soon turbulence passes and all is still.
Across the deep sea of stars they sail.
And our little Emmy is no longer pale.

Ahead an airliner appears in the sky.
That's no surprise. Airliners can fly.
The reindeer soar high over the craft.
A passengers sees—thinks himself daft.

Moonshadows of deer slide over the wing,
a breathtaking and a beautiful thing.
That passenger will arrive home tonight
holding in his heart a brand-new light.

The plane is gone, the North Pole looms.
The sleigh arcs down. The reindeer *zoom*
toward a hard, endless, icy wasteland.
"Emmy," says Lottie, "give me your hand!"

Straight down, down, and down some more.
"There's going to be such blood and gore,"
squeals Emmy. "Oh, we're going to crash!"
But one reindeer says, "Don't be so rash.

"Believe in Santa and look down again.
Believing makes the difference, so then
you'll see Santa's village spread below
a wonderland of light and ice and snow."

"I see it," says Emmy, "oh, I really do!"
"I see it, I see it!" Charlotte says too.
Cottages, lamplight, and gleaming spires,
colorful lights on invisible wires.

Trees hung with icing, gingerbread shrubs,
bottled root beer in street-corner tubs,
movie theaters where shows play for free,
with popcorn and ice cream. Oh, golly gee!

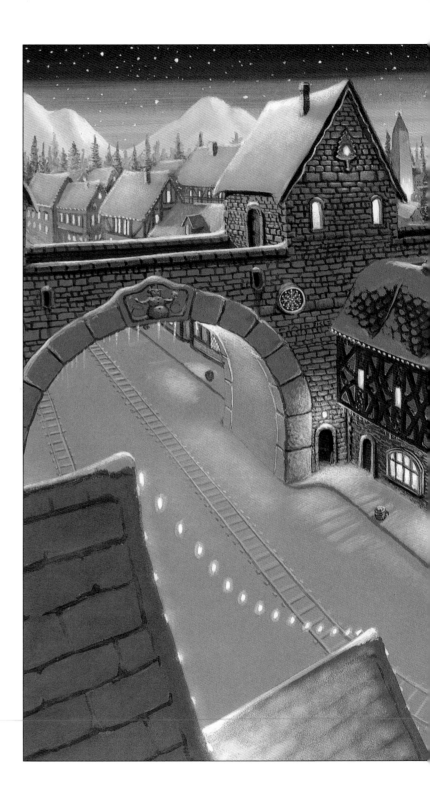

The reindeer land on their delicate feet,
racing swiftly along the glittering street
to the golden heart of the village square,
to the house of houses standing there.

No doubt it's the house of Santa Claus.
The girls recognize it at once, because
Carved over the door in a lintel of wood:
HE KNOWS IF YOU'VE BEEN BAD OR GOOD.

The village seems deserted, eerily quiet.
A dropping pin would sound like a riot.
No sign at all of the toy-making elves.
Where might they have taken themselves?

A reindeer says, "Their good work is done.
Now they're all on vacation, having fun.
In Tahiti, Jamaica, Pittsburgh, and France.
Some to Texas: They like to square-dance."

"Where's Mrs. Claus?" Emmy asks with awe.
"Bernice?" says a deer. "She's at a spa
in California. Somewhere on the coast.
bathing in the sun, as brown as toast.

"Santa always joins her on Christmas Day.
It's their once-a-year chance to get away.
By the middle of January they come back
to start filling next year's big toy sack."

Lottie and Emmy spring from the sleigh,
dashing to Santa's house straightaway.
The door is ajar. Blame the bad twin.
They push it open and dare to go in.

A hallway glows with warm twinkly light,
gilded, coffered, paneled—just right.
No sign of Santa. But there's some mud
the bad twin tracked in. Then—a thud!

𝒜 thud from the cellar far down below.
No time to waste. The two girls go
to a massively timbered door they spy,
and down the cellar stairs they fly.

Down, down, around, and down some more
in lantern light to a cold stone floor.
A huge burlap bag, spotted with grime:
This is it—the scene of the crime!

Untie the knot! Quick, open the sack!
Santa's inside! Pull the burlap back!
Off with the blindfold! And the gag!
Off with these ropes! Out of the bag!

He jumps to his feet, almost topples,
steadies himself, pops his ear stopples.
"Dear girls! How well you have behaved!
Without you Christmas couldn't be saved."

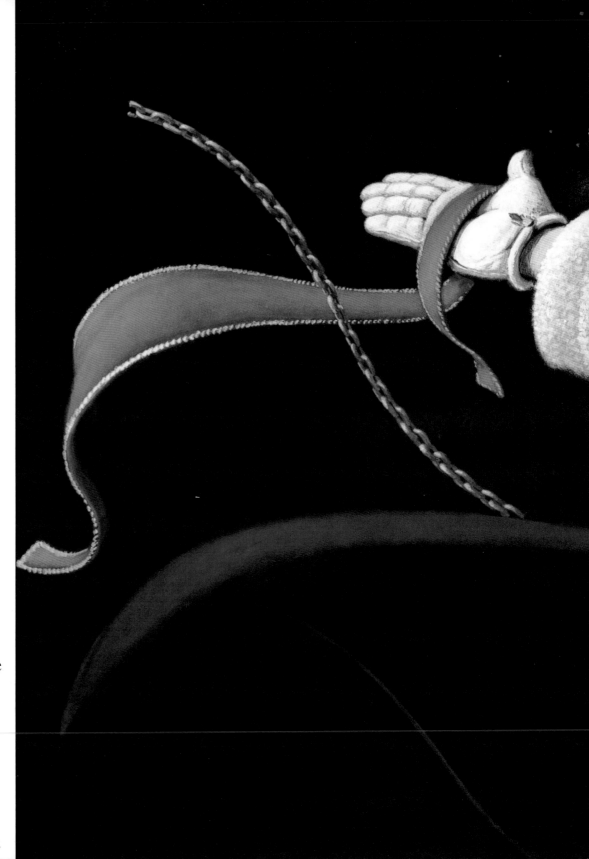

Oh, *this* is Santa, no doubt about that.
From his boots to the pom-pom on his hat,
  he's radiant, glorious, a sight to behold,
  the elf about whom so many tales are told.
He laughs—*ho ho ho!* His merry eyes shine.
His sweet, kindly smile is simply divine.

"You're Emily. And Charlotte. I know you.
  You're two good girls, through and through.
  I've never had to bring you lumps of coal
  on one of my annual trips from the Pole.
Those were magic ropes, blindfold, and gag.
Only good kids could free me from that bag."

Says Emmy, "The bad Claus is in the sleigh,
  tied up tight. Now let's be on our way.
We must save Christmas—it's getting late."
Lottie says, "Hold on a minute. Just wait.
  I'm wondering why, at this magical Pole
  your cellar is such a deep, dark hole."

Santa winces, sighs. "Also dismal and dank.
  And when we first moved in, it really stank.
We have a problem with ground-water seepage
and really persistent purple fungus creepage.
Girls, everyone has troubles, even Saint Nick.
  So smile and be merry. That's the trick!"

Back in the square in front of the house,
the little stuffed toys unload the louse
who's wrapped up in jump ropes and Slinkys,
his mustache still secured to his pinkies.
He's wide awake now and not half so fearful.
The real Santa Claus gives him an earful.

"What in the world were you trying to do?
Surely you're not bad through and through.
Confused, misguided, no doubt about that.
You wear my suit well—especially the hat.
Always be nice to kids, give 'em a smile.
They'll all love you too—after a while."

Emmy says, "Be nice, as you were taught.
When you're bad, you'll *always* be caught.
What if we told your mom what you've done,
then would being bad really be much fun?"
Lottie says, "You even hit me with a pie.
If your mom knew it all, wouldn't she cry?"

Emmy shakes her finger. "Oh, shame on you.
Don't you know before everything you do,
you must ask yourself how Mom would feel
to know you'd done it? That's the seal
of approval and the guidance we all need
to help us be good and to do good deeds."

The bad Claus's eyes well up with tears.
He sniffles, then blubbers, when he hears
the girls mention Mother. "Oh, please!
But for the Slinkys, I'd be on my knees,
begging you not to tell dear Mama Claus
all the bad things I've done, because

"she's the sweetest and kindest of souls
you'll ever find between the two poles.
I've been thoughtless, so mean and bad.
But I never wanted to make Mama sad.
I've been as bad as a bad boy could be
because I never thought Mama would see."

Lottie says, "No one can fool his mother
any more than kids can fool your brother.
Sooner or later every mom always knows
if you've been bad or good. It shows.
Scary, I know, but that's how it goes.
Now stop blubbering and wipe your nose."

Snow begins to fall from the polar skies
as Santa says, "Girls, you are both wise.
I'm giving you two brand-new blue bikes
and to your parents—whatever each likes.
And you will come along to share the joy
as I bring gifts to every girl and boy."

Un-Slinky'd, with all jump ropes unwound,
Santa's brother leaps up from the ground.
"Let's hurry and undo all that I've done,
or this year Christmas won't be much fun."

A crowded sleigh—two Clauses, two girls—
rockets into the sky as the snow swirls.
"Good reindeer, I'm sorry for all I said.
I had the meanies, shoulda stayed in bed."
So explains the previously twisted twin,
who's better now than he's recently been.

Lottie and Emmy are afraid that the crime
can't be undone. There's too little time.
But Santa can deliver in a single hour,
by stretching time with his magical power.

Flying like a comet, chased by the sun,
they sneak past every police radar gun.
The best trick of all: At any one time,
they can be in many places—oh, 9009.
How this is possible no one explains,
leaving the girls with headache pains.

At last all gifts have been given away,
and still night hasn't turned into day.
They race the sun to the girls' place,
where soon it's time for them to face
Mom and Dad on the snowy front lawn.
Someone might be spanked before dawn.

Pouring out through the open front door
is popcorn. And from a few windows—more.
Popcorn has popped from the chimney too.
"Oh, what a terrible thing did I do?"
asks the once-bad Claus, who now behaves.
"Ten pounds of corn and some microwaves

"can do more damage than I ever thought.
Gee, I have to admit I was never taught
to be such a mischievous fat old elf.
I'm totally, thoroughly ashamed of myself.
Girls, I'll see that you're both thanked.
If anyone is, *I'll* be the one spanked."

Down to the front yard the reindeer fly.
Mom and Dad are waiting to be told why
their house has become a popcorn machine,
waking them from their Christmas dreams.
They stand in pajamas, robes, and slippers,
gazing up at their sleigh-flying nippers.

From the sleigh into Mom and Dad's arms,
both girls use their clever-child charms
to keep Santa's brother from being paddled.
"Forgive him. He was temporarily addled.
But he helped put Christmas back on track.
He'll never again stuff Santa in a sack."

Santa says, "I'm Santa and this is my twin.
His name is Bob. Will you let us come in
to clean up the mess, set everything right,
before dawn puts an end to this magic night?
Your house is the last stop on our journeys,
and I sincerely hope we can avoid attorneys."

With mouths wide open as if to catch flies,
Mom and Dad gaze at the sleigh, the skies.
The sight of the red-suited smiling Clauses
leaves their eyes wide and apparently causes
an attack of whim-whams. They can't speak.
Dad softly peeps, Mom squeaks a small squeak.

Santa says, "I'll assume the answer is yes."
Then he and Bob, in three minutes or less,
Vaporize all the popcorn, clean up the mud,
magically transform the toad snot and crud
into gifts that are sure to please everyone
and ensure Christmas morning is nonstop fun.

Out in the front yard, each girl gets a hug
from each of the Clauses. Cute as a bug—
each girl, that is. Well, each Claus too.
Bob says, "I left a big brown cow for you,
prettily gift-wrapped, by one of the trees."
Then Santa wants to turn Bob over his knee.

Bob says, "Giving a cow—that's not mean.
Remember, with milk we can make ice cream!"
Santa gives his brother a very stern look,
and Bob decides to operate more by the book.
"Okay, so I'll change the cow into a guppy.
Better yet, make it a small black puppy."

Then into the big sleigh each Claus bounds.
Mom and Dad are still making curious sounds:
gasps of surprise and squeaks and peeps.
What is the particular problem that keeps
grown-ups from accepting that magic is real,
that it's okay to believe in what you *feel?*

Into the night, eight reindeer take flight.
The big soaring sleigh is a wondrous sight.
Then Santa and Bob call out from on high:
"Yo, Lottie! Yo, Emmy! Goodbye, goodbye!
Believing in magic, you saved Christmas Day.
Keep believing in us after we've gone away!"

$\mathcal{N}$ow that you have finished this book,
turn the pages, take a second look.
In every picture you are sure to see
a jolly snowman peering back at thee.
Some of our snowmen are easy to spot,
but many among them simply are not.
Hiding, lurking—but none are mean—
they're keeping an eye on the scene.
You see, snowmen work for the Claus,
reporting to the North Pole because
Santa must know who's good or not,
so he can avoid delivering toad snot
to all good children who deserve toys.
Santa is fair to all girls and boys.
Never be mean or  say something untrue,
because a snowman may be watching you.